This Little Tiger book belongs to:

_____

_____

_____

THIS WAY →

For Maxine

LITTLE TIGER PRESS
An imprint of Magi Publications
1 The Coda Centre, 189 Munster Road, London SW6 6AW
www.littletigerpress.com

First published in Great Britain 2006
This edition published 2006

Text and illustrations copyright © Matt Buckingham 2006
Matt Buckingham has asserted his right to be identified
as the author and illustrator of this work
under the Copyright, Designs and Patents Act, 1988

A CIP catalogue record for this book is available
from the British Library

Printed in China

6 8 10 9 7

Bright Stanley

Matt Buckingham

LITTLE TIGER PRESS
London

Far below the waves a little fish called
Stanley lived with his shoal.
They were the brightest, sparkliest fish
in the whole of the deep, dark sea.

One morning Stanley
woke up rather late.
"Coo-ee! It's me-ee!"
he called to his friends.
But the reef seemed
strangely quiet.

Suddenly Stanley remembered that
today was the day when the shoal
swam to cooler waters for the summer.
"Jumping jellyfish!" he groaned.
He hurried to the Meeting Point
as fast as his fins could carry him.
But there was no one there.

As he looked around
he saw a bright light.
"A-ha, they haven't
got far!" he said and
he raced towards it.

But it was only a lobster counting coins.
"Go away! Don't touch my treasure!" the
lobster growled, snip-snapping his claws.
"I'm just looking for my friends," said Stanley.

"Fish!" the lobster grumbled. "Those others were in such a hurry to find someone they upset my coins."
"Others?" cried Stanley. "My friends!"
"Well, go and join them then," said the lobster, pointing grumpily, and Stanley sped off.

Ahead of him Stanley
saw a golden glow.
He could just make
out a bright, sparkly
fish. One of his friends!
"Coo-ee! It's me-ee!"
he called, swimming
even faster.

CLONK!

Stanley crashed head-first
into something very hard.

"Jumping jellyfish!" he cried. It wasn't one of his friends at all, but his own reflection in a shiny pearl!

Stanley rubbed his bumped nose, feeling a little dazed. He didn't notice a dark shape coming up behind him.

When he turned round Stanley found himself staring straight into the mouth of a huge . . .

"AAARGH!" shrieked Stanley. Over boulders and under weeds he dashed with the shark snapping at his tail.

Suddenly Stanley saw a small hole in a rock below. He dived down and wriggled inside, just before he was gobbled up.

Deep inside the cave, Stanley shivered and shook. He felt very sad and very lonely. He was beginning to think he'd never see his friends again.

"Well, I can't stay here for ever," he sighed at last and he poked his head out of the cave to check that the shark had gone.

"Jumping jellyfish!"
he squealed.
    The sea was a golden
orange, sparkling and
glittering. It was the most
wonderful sight he had
ever seen because there,
in front of him, was . . .

. . . his shoal!

"Coo-ee! It's me-ee!" he called.

"Stanley!" his friends shouted. "Where have you been? We've been looking for you everywhere!"

And Stanley told them his adventures as they all swam off in one bright, sparkly, happy shoal.